DATE DUE

The Mess

Note

Once a reader can recognize and identify the 20 words used to tell this story, he or she will be able to read successfully the entire book. These 20 words are repeated throughout the story, so that young readers will be able to easily recognize the words and understand their meaning.

The 20 words used in this book are:

a	friends	made	run
can	go	mess	slide
cannot	hide	my	the
clean	I	outside	then
down	I'll	play	today

Library of Congress Cataloging-in-Publication Data
Jensen, Patricia.
    The mess/by Patricia Jensen; illustrated by Molly Delaney.
       p.   cm—(My first reader)
    Summary: Forbidden to go outside because his room is a mess, a young boy reflects on the pleasures he is missing.
        Previously published by Grolier.
        ISBN 0-516-05357-4
        (1. Play—Fiction. 2. Orderliness—Fiction. 3. Stories in rhyme.) I. Delaney, Molly, ill. II. Title. III. Series.
PZ8.3.J424Me 1990
(E)—dc20

90-30158
CIP
AC

The Mess

Written by Patricia Jensen   *Illustrated by Molly Delaney*

ↀP CHILDRENS PRESS ®

CHICAGO

Text © 1990 Nancy Hall, Inc. Illustrations © Molly Delaney.
All rights reserved. Published by Childrens Press®, Inc.
Printed in the United States of America. Published simultaneously in Canada.
Developed by Nancy Hall, Inc. Designed by Antler & Baldwin Design Group.

1 2 3 4 5 6 7 8 9 10 R 99 98 97 96 95 94 93 92 91

I cannot go

outside today.

I made a mess.

I cannot play.

I cannot run.

13

I cannot hide.

I cannot go

slide down the slide.

My friends can run.

My friends can hide.

My friends can go

slide down the slide.

I'll clean the mess!

Then I can play!

Then I can go
outside today!